The Golden Ass

The Golden Ass

of

Lucius Apuleius
Romæ · circa a.d. CL

Now a Book for Young Readers of All Ages

ADAPTED FROM THE LATIN ORIGINAL BY

M. D. Usher

ILLUSTRATIONS BY

T. Motley

David R. Godine · *Publisher*

BOSTON

First published in 2011 by
DAVID R. GODINE · *Publisher*
Post Office Box 450
Jaffrey, New Hampshire 03452
www.godine.com

LIBRARY OF CONGRESS
CATALOGING-IN-PUBLICATION DATA

Usher, Mark David, 1966–
The golden ass of Lucius Apuleius : now a book for young readers
of all ages / adapted from the Latin original by M. D. Usher ;
illustrations by T. Motley.
p. cm.
ISBN 978-1-56792-418-3 (hardcover)
[1. Metamorphosis—Fiction. 2. Magic—Fiction. 3. Social classes—
Fiction. 4. Mythology, Classical—Fiction.] I. Motley, Tom, ill.
II. Apuleius. Metamorphoses. III. Title.
PZ7.U6955Gol 2011
[Fic]—dc22
2010032978

FIRST PRINTING
Printed in China

CONTENTS

CUI DONO LEPIDVM NOVVM LIBELLVM?

ROBBIE MAYES, TIBI: NAMQUE TU SOLEBAS
MEAS ESSE ALIQUID PUTARE NUGAS,

ET

KATE ROBINSON SCHVBART,
LECTORI DOCTÆ VENVSTÆQUE

The Golden Ass

I was on my way to Thessaly . . .

CHAPTER I

The Road to Larissa

I T WAS AN awful trip, full of twists, turns, thickets and thorns. I was on my way to Thessaly for business, and was plodding along on horseback. The sun was scorching. My backside bristled like a pincushion from sitting so long in the saddle. It looked, too, as if my poor horse could use a rest. So I hopped down, unhitched his bridle, and gave him some water from my pigskin flask. Then – suddenly – just as I was about to take a long swig myself, I heard a coughball of laughter erupt from behind me, as if someone were clearing his throat.

"*Procul, profane, mendacia ista . . .*" said a raspy voice in provincial Latin. "Get out of here, you little rascal! Stop telling such outrageous and ridiculous LIES!"

Startled, I looked up to see two strange figures traipsing

round the bend. One was short, hairy, and fat; the other –
a boy – tall, smooth, and thin. This strange spectacle in itself
caught my attention, but being curious by nature, and slightly
giddy from the heat, I was eager to know just what they had
been talking about. (I fancied myself an educated man –
a recent graduate of Plato's Academy, no less – and thought
that, by and large, I was in a good position to judge for myself
whether something was false or true.)

"Excuse me, sir," I said to the short hairy man. "Perhaps I
can be of some assistance. Just what do you find so unbeliev-
able about your young friend's story?" (It was obvious they
had been talking about it for some time.) "I don't even know
what you were talking about, but I do know that things aren't
always what they seem. All the philosophers teach us THAT.
And people often disbelieve what happens only seldom or
what they cannot comprehend."

I scratched my head to try to think of a good example of
what I meant.

"I'm reminded of the time I choked on an olive at a dinner
party," I added. "I was just eating as usual when all of a sudden
an olive got stuck in my throat. I turned green, purple, red, then
pale before I managed to hock that thing up again. I thought it
was the end of me. Just one tiny olive! Yet the very next day I
saw a performer at the circus slide a huge sword down HIS
throat. For him, it was no trouble at all. And, to top it off, when
he pulled it back out again, the sword-blade had disappeared

and a bouquet of flowers was attached to the hilt! It was quite a feat, and based on my own harrowing experience with that olive the night before, I could scarcely believe my eyes.

"Besides," I continued, turning to the boy, "I've had no company or human conversation for days – only this horse here. So please, go on with your tale, young man. Say, the three of us could travel together. Are you heading to Larissa?"

The two of them stood silent, stumped, I supposed, by my essay on the olive. I thought a moment about a way to win them over and sweeten the deal.

"I'll tell you what," I added after this uncomfortable pause. "If you agree to finish your story, young man, I'll treat you both to dinner at the inn when we arrive."

"Now THAT sounds like a fine proposition indeed!" said the fat man roundly, rubbing his belly. "But you yourself had better lay off the olives, Sir."

"And it would be nice to have my story fall on friendly ears," said the boy, warming to me, but glaring at his squat companion, "FOR NOT A WORD OF IT IS UNTRUE!"

"Cylindrius, at your service," said the fat man. "I'm the boy's tutor."

"Pleased to meet you," I said as I doubled over to shake his stubby hand.

"And I'm Prudentius," said the boy. "What's your name?"

"Lucius," I said. "Lucius Apuleius. I've come from Rome on business."

"Well, Master Lucius," Cylindrius replied, "even your swordsman at the circus would have a hard time swallowing the story of Prudentius here."

"Let the gentleman hear my story and decide for himself!" Prudentius retorted.

Cylindrius winced, but I eagerly nodded my assent. And so it was we set off down the road again, and the boy resumed his tale.

CHAPTER II

Milo the Millionaire

"ABOUT A year ago to the day," Prudentius began, "I was traveling this very road to Larissa, like you, on business. I used to be a successful wine salesman, you see, and I needed a loan in order to expand my operations to the northern Empire."

"Now wait a minute," I jumped in. "How can you have been a wine salesman? You're scarcely eleven years old!"

"I'm twelve, actually," Prudentius objected. "Listen to my story through TO THE END and you'll soon understand. OK?"

"OK," I said, eager for the rest.

"Anyhow," Prudentius continued, "in Larissa there lives a man by the name of Milo, a self-made millionaire who lends money to enterprising fellows like himself. He lends at high

7

interest, to be sure, but I had exhausted all my sources of credit at Rome, and so I had little choice. Plus, I came to Milo with a sparkling letter of introduction from a mutual friend of ours named Demeas:

DEMEAS TO MILO THE MILLIONAIRE:

GREETINGS! The bearer of this letter, one Prudentius Honestus Maximus, is a remarkable young man, full of intelligence, energy, and wit. I recommend him to you without reservation. His only fault seems to be that he is rarely content with minding his own business. Rather, he is always prying into the businesses of others.

Milo the money-lender smiled broadly when he read that last line. It was apparently a sentiment close to his millionaire's heart and secured my hospitable welcome.

"Prying into the businesses of others, indeed!" he chuckled. "Now, THAT'S what makes men rich, Prudentius!"

Without looking up, Milo snapped his fingers and a throng of servants scurried to the hems of his toga.

"Xanthus, prepare a banquet for our visitor here," he bellowed.

"Phidippides, take his bags to the guest quarters. And Bibulus, for the gods' sake, get this young man something to drink."

"And some hay for my horse, please?" I added meekly. "He's had quite a journey too." (You see, I always made a point of looking after my horse.)

"Yes, your horse. Of course," said Milo, twirling his baubled finger in the direction of yet another servant. My horse whinnied his approval.

"You will join me for dinner, Prudentius," he groaned as he pushed his gargantuan frame up from his chair, "at sunset."

Milo then hobbled down the hallway, supported by two small servant girls, who looked less like girls than sparrows flitting about a lumbering elephant on the African plain. I shook my head and had a second look to be sure I wasn't imagining things.

Here I need to make a confession. Thessaly, you see, is a country famous for all things strange and supernatural. In Thessaly, they say, all the women are witches and all the men magicians. I myself had had a long fascination with magic, and that was part of my reason for coming here in the first place. Magic, I was told, can change the course of rivers, subdue a raging sea, throttle the winds, and stop the sun in its tracks; it can make the moon reverse the ocean's tides, pluck stars from the sky, obliterate a day, or prolong a night. That's nothing to sneer at, especially if you're in business.

In any event, that's what made me think twice about Milo's appearance. Was he a shape-shifter? I rubbed my eyes, and when I came back to my senses, I made my way down the hall and wasted no time in getting to my room.

There, I immediately ransacked the closets and drawers, curious to see if there was anything a previous guest had left behind, or if Milo had left some treat or magical trinket somewhere in the room unawares. To my great disappointment, there were no such goods to be found, so I collapsed, exhausted, on the bed and slept like a baby on Milo's silk pillows and luxurious sheets.

Dinner that evening was equally delightful: Roasted boar, anchovy tenderloins, stuffed pigeons, candied chestnuts, melons, and tarts. The only damper on the evening was that Milo had the oddly vulgar habit of belching out loud, laughing uncontrollably, then wiping his nose on his sleeve.

"No, my wife does not approve of my manners," he giggled, red-faced, sensing my disgust. "But she's not here, is she?" he added with a wink and a nod.

"Where IS your wife, Milo?" I asked politely.

"Who knows?" he belched again, laughing. "That witch is probably off concocting something or other."

"I see," I said. There was obviously some bad blood between Milo and his wife, so I figured it was just as well that she hadn't joined us for dinner.

The evening wore on in much the same fashion, with Milo belching, giggling, winking and nodding. Just when I thought I couldn't take any more, Phidippides came with a torch to lead me back to my room. I gushed with the usual courtesies, compliments and thank-you's, then hurried down the hall to my room, where, to my sheer delight, a servant had already prepared a hot bath.

AH! OH! The steamy water turned all my tired muscles to mush. Soon my thoughts began to drift to the whopping loan that I imagined Milo would offer me in the morning. I was on my way to becoming the biggest and the richest wine seller in Rome! Not bad for an orphan. (I had, you see, lost my parents in a shipwreck off the coast of Egypt when I was eight.)

It was in the midst of these reveries that it dawned on me again just where I was – in the heart of Thessaly, land of wizards and witchcraft.

What did Milo mean by that comment about his wife? How could I be sure Milo was truly himself and not the elephant he so closely resembled? (Or the pig he seemed at dinner?) And were those in fact servant girls, or sparrows, at his side? What had I just eaten for supper?! My blood ran cold and the anchovy tenderloins sat uneasily in the pit of my stomach.

Just then a mysterious silhouette caught my eye through the open window.

I climbed out of the bath, crouched down, and tip-toed over for a better view. There were TWO silhouettes, one vaguely reminiscent of Milo himself, but wearing a dress, the other small and shapely. As the figures moved into the lamp light,

I stood shivering from the eerie beauty of what I had seen.

it became clear that they were both women – Milo's wife, I supposed, and a servant girl.

The girl was nervously sorting through a long shelf of earthenware containers, occasionally tipping one over, then clumsily putting it back into place. Milo's wife, meanwhile, her back turned to me, had slipped out of her clothes and was mumbling something unintelligible under her breath.

"Bring me the ointment!" she interrupted herself in stately Latin. The girl grabbed a canister from the shelf and started over to her mistress, tripping once or twice along the way.

Milo's wife took the small pot and began smearing an iridescent blue lotion over her body, chanting once again in some barbarian tongue, when suddenly, POOF!, a fast flutter of wings and a shriek was all that was left of her, and she soared, a snowy white owl, out of the window and into the night.

I stood there dumbfounded, dripping wet and shivering from the eerie beauty of what I had seen – or what I THOUGHT I had seen. I jumped quickly under the covers, my mind racing with thoughts for the morning, and tried to fall asleep.

CHAPTER III

Owls and Asses

EVER IN my life had I been so eager to get up out of bed. Scarcely had the cock crowed than I was washed, dressed, and on my way to the site of that glorious transformation the night before.

I made my way through the labyrinth of Milo's sprawling house until I came to the women's quarters across the courtyard from my bedroom. This was the place, I was sure, and I tugged vigorously at the door handle.

It was locked.

Just when I was preparing for a second round of tugging, I heard a sweet, melodious voice behind me.

"Excuse me, Sir. What are you doing?"

Embarrassed, I turned around and smiled, my hands

folded behind my back: It was the servant girl I had seen the night before. What luck! What good fortune! I thought to myself.

"Well, hello there, Miss," I started. "I'm a salesman specializing in jars and ointments. Milo, your master, has hired me to take an inventory of all jars and canisters containing ointment in this home," I lied, "and this is the only room I have not yet inspected. Do you perchance have a key?"

"But these are my mistress's private chambers," she said innocently. "No one's allowed in there 'cept her."

"Well, I can certainly appreciate your respect for your mistress," I replied. "Like you, I too am just following orders. And, like you, I'd be the last person to disobey them. In fact, I'll bet if we got to know one another better, we'd find we had a lot in common, you and I. As they say," I said with the wink and the nod I had picked up from Milo the night before, "birds of a feather flock together, if you know what I mean."

The poor, innocent girl did not follow my meaning, but proceeded to unlock the door anyway on the strength of my spurious credentials as a jar inspector. My heart was pounding – both from telling such a monstrous lie and at the prospects of being let into the room.

The girl fumbled with what seemed like a thousand keys and made such a noise over it all that I thought for sure we would attract someone's attention.

Finally, we were in. I shut the door firmly behind us and

headed straight for the long shelf of earthenware jars. I was so beside myself with curiosity that I had completely forgotten about my breakfast meeting with Milo about the loan.

"Quite a collection you have here," I said, running my fingers over each canister and pretending to take notes. "This one's exquisite. And THAT one – why, I haven't seen one like THAT this side of Corinth. Now, which one contains the blue ointment?" I added bluntly.

The girl gave me a puzzled look and pointed to a squat jar at the far end of the shelf. Trembling with excitement, I grabbed the jar, threw off my tunic and began smearing the lotion all over my body.

"Oh dear!" the girl gasped, realizing now my true intentions. "You shouldn't be doing that, Sir!"

"Oh, it's quite alright," I said. "You see, I saw you here with your mistress the other night when she turned herself into an owl – "

As I was talking and rubbing, I felt a strange sensation and heard a loud BOING! – yes, it was distinctly a BOING! and not the POOF! I had heard the previous night –

" – and I thought I'd try her trick out for myself," I continued, rubbing away. "I'm very keen on magic, you see."

"But you need to recite the spell AFTER DARK!" the girl exclaimed with a worried look on her face.

My jaw dropped: SPELL? DARK? What had I done?! Suddenly, I felt my ears begin to stretch and itch. When I

You shouldn't be doing that, Sir!

reached up to scratch them, I noticed that my arms were covered with hair and my fingers had hardened into hooves! Then my nose started tingling and twitching till, BOING!, it popped into the shape of a snout! My bottom, too, bristled and throbbed, then, BOING!, out flopped a tail! I had turned myself into . . . a donkey!

Twisting this way and that as the magic ointment worked its way through my body, I knocked over the shelf. The whole collection of pots fell to the floor with a tremendous crash.

The servant girl covered her mouth and partially swallowed a scream. I, on the other hand, opened my mouth as wide as I could to cry for help. Out came the HE, but there was no HELP on the way, only a HAW. "HE-HAW!" I croaked. "HE-HAW!"

"Oh NO!" gasped the girl. "You've made an ass of yourself!" And indeed I had.

CHAPTER IV

Caught in the Act

ANTHUS heard all this commotion in the women's quarters and came running with his toga tucked up to his knees. The girl, meanwhile, had slipped away, fearing the consequences – as well she might – of being caught with an ass in her mistress's room. I was all alone, surrounded by broken pots and pools of the finest magical potions in the world. Xanthus skidded to a stop in front of the door.

"Great gods above, how did YOU get in here?" he scolded. "Back to the stables with you!"

"Wait, it's me, Milo's house guest, Prudentius," I yearned to say. But all that came out of my mouth was an ugly snort.

"Being ornery, are we?" Xanthus scowled. "Bibulus," he shouted, "fetch a stick!"

When I saw Bibulus trotting down the hall with a stick large enough to slay the Minotaur, I whimpered to myself, "Oh please, not THAT!" (After all, I may have had the body and speech of an ass, but my mind was still fully human.)

Fearing the stick, I lowered my ears, tail between my legs, and went reluctantly out to the stables.

As Fate would have it, Xanthus put me into the same stall as my own horse. At first, I thought this a brilliant stroke of good luck, assuming that there must be some unspoken bond in the animal kingdom between horses and mules, or that, with my horse's keen scent, he might recognize his gentle master inside this donkey's hide. But as soon as Xanthus was gone, my trusty steed lowered his head and gave me such a kick that it sent me tumbling to the corner of the stall. (I've since learned the truth about the word ASSUME: it only makes an ASS out of U and ME.)

"This is MY hay!" my horse seemed to be saying. And not liking hay much myself, I wasn't about to argue.

Oh wretched me! This was, hands and hooves down, the worst day in my life! I had been changed into an ass and rejected by my own horse! Plus, I had missed my breakfast business meeting with Milo. I licked the salty tear that rolled down my now furry cheek.

"If you can hear me in there, Sir," a sweet, melodious voice chirped through a chink in the wall, "the antidote to your spell is to eat roses."

I knew that voice – it was the servant girl! She had come back for me!

"I found the recipe in my mistress's parchments, and though I don't read very well myself, it's hard not to understand a picture of a rose. And don't you worry, Sir, your secret is safe with me." The girl flashed me a heartwarming smile, then scampered off back to the house.

Secret? SECRET? I, Prudentius Honestus Maximus, wanted the whole wide WORLD to know that I had been mistakenly transformed into an ass!

ROSES, I thought. I had to find some roses – and quickly, before my jealous horse decided to kick me again over the hay.

I spent the rest of the afternoon gnawing through a slat on the wooden gate of my stall and eventually squeezed my way past. By this time it was getting dark, so I went directly to Milo's garden in search of a rose bush. And there, shining in the moonlight, was a whole garland of freshly cut roses draped over a statue of the goddess Diana.

Well that wasn't too difficult, I thought, quite pleased with myself. I leaned over, closed my eyes, and just as I was about to munch a delicious blossom –

"Over here! There's an ass over here in the garden!" someone shouted close behind me.

There's an ass over here in the garden!

All of a sudden, the sound of barking dogs, screaming women and rattling swords punched me in the ears. I looked up from my roses and saw Milo streaking through the courtyard, waving his arms: Bandits had broken into the house and were carrying away his possessions!

I immediately did what donkeys do best when faced with adversity: I rolled over and played dead. But this didn't work: A rough hand cinched a noose around my neck, yanked me to my feet and out into the courtyard. Then, one by one, a chorus line of bandits began to toss large objects onto my back – couches and bathtubs and chests full of silver and gold. My knees buckled under the load.

"Yah, mule!" wheezed one toothless criminal, grinning ear to ear.

Still dazed by this sudden turn of events, I tottered off, driven by curses and sticks – as Fate would have it – from the house of a money-lender to a den of thieves.

CHAPTER V

A Den of Thieves

S IF BANDITS *per se* were not bad enough, these marauders made their home not on the pleasant steppes of Thessaly, or on the sandy shores of the wine-dark sea, but in a desolate, despicable cave at the peak of Mount Olympus. Up, up, up we climbed, over rocks, roots, and stumps. Vultures hovered close overhead, and Zeus himself was gathering storm clouds on high. Burdened with thoughts of my former self (not to mention the entire contents of Milo's house on my back), I felt like Atlas carrying the weight of the world.

The vast cave was home to a whole city of thieves. Bandits were coming and going, merrily slapping one another on the back, cursing and spitting. Those who had stayed behind wept as they welcomed their brother bandits home from the raid like heroes returning from Troy. I rolled my eyes with a mixture of disbelief and exhaustion.

After their silly hugging ritual was over, the thieves finally began to unload the couches, bathtubs and chests, then tied me up in the corner of the cave. Someone even tossed me a forkful of hay, but I couldn't bring myself to eat it. All I could think about were roses, or at least some good sausages, olives, or cheese – anything but hay, which I had never eaten in my life, and I wasn't about to start eating now.

The delicious smell of roasting meat and barley wine wafting from the bandits' celebration feast tortured me all through the night. And I shuddered to hear them boast about their evil deeds. In the morning, I overheard them say, they intended to set out to kidnap a young princess from Pydna and to pull out all her pretty fingernails one by one until her father paid the ransom.

"And then maybe we'll just kill 'er anyhow!" one of the criminals squealed with delight.

I shuddered again. Poor princess! I thought as I bedded down on my hay. Poor Prudentius!

When Dawn had spread her rosy fingers across the sky, the bandits began to wake up from their drunken slumber. After some hot disagreements and grumpy, early morning disputes, they eventually set off for Pydna.

This was my chance! I champed through my rope and

I felt like Atlas carrying the weight of the world.

bounded down the side of the mountain like a stallion running after a company of mares. I ran and ran and RAN. I was so exhilarated by my escape that I momentarily forgot myself and my sorry predicament. Finally, I stopped and came to my senses: ROSES, I panted, out of breath.

I looked up and saw a small garden attached to a shepherd's hut. What luck! I thought. I leapt over the stone wall in a single bound and surveyed my surroundings, but there was not a rose in sight, not even some inedible mountain variety. Instead, there were rows and rows of cabbages, lettuce, and beans. By this time I was weak and practically delirious with hunger, so I sat down amongst the cabbages and ate and ate until I could eat no more.

Now one of the advantages of being an ass is that you have enormous ears and are able to catch wind of approaching sounds while they're still far off in the distance. One of the DISadvantages is that once you've made yourself comfortable in a shepherd's cabbage patch and eaten most of his crop, it's hard to get up very quickly. Thus, by the time I recognized the faint sound of barking dogs and human voices, it was too late: the shepherd had already burst out of his hut carrying an axe, followed by his wife, who wielded a hot iron.

"CERBERUS!" the wife whistled loudly. Out came a monstrous dog, snarling and curling his lips. THIS sent me to my feet in a hurry: I charged through the garden and bashed down the gate with my hoof.

All day long I was chased across the forested peaks of Olympus, hunted like a stag by the shepherd, his wife, and their dog. When they were so close that I could feel Cerberus's hot breath on my heels, I suddenly felt horribly ill. Much to my pursuers' surprise, I stopped dead in my tracks, my stomach bloated and distended. Then, quite involuntarily, I lifted my tail and let go with a frightening explosion of gas.

As any human knows, boiled cabbage is one thing, but a dozen heads of raw cabbage on an empty stomach was more than my system could bear. In fact, as a newly minted donkey, my system wasn't even accustomed to hay!

That was the end of the shepherd, his wife and their dog. They retreated to their hut, gagging and gasping for breath.

By now it was getting dark and cold on the mountain. Not knowing where else to go, I returned to the cave and fell fast asleep on my bed of hay.

Later that night the bandits also returned. I was awakened by a muffled thump on the ground in my corner. I looked up and, by the light of a torch, caught sight of the prettiest face I had ever seen in my life.

CHAPTER VI

Princess Charity

"Now, DON'T get any ideas, Princess!" barked a filthy, one-eyed villain. "You try to escape and it's" – the bandit laughed as he jerked his finger across his throat with an obscene gesture.

The proud princess kept her composure and looked the other way. But once her captor was gone, she burst into tears. She sobbed uncontrollably – the kind of deep, pitiful sobs any young girl would succumb to if she had been snatched from her family and was being held against her will by bandits in a disgusting cave with an ass. I inched over and placed my muzzle in her lap to try to cheer her up.

"Oh, what a kind, considerate donkey!" she exclaimed, stroking my forehead.

If only you could talk!

I batted my eyelashes, and gazed longingly up at her beautiful face.

"If only you could talk! But, oh," she hesitated, "your BREATH! Is that cabbage I smell?"

Blushing, I sat up, so as not to offend, and the princess, for lack of any human companionship, proceeded to tell me her whole story. She spoke as if I understood every word (which, of course, I did): How her name was Charity, and how she had been kidnapped on her wedding day at the very moment she was about to kiss her new husband; how the bandits dragged her by the hair from the altar of Aphrodite, tearing her brand new saffron-colored dress; how her bridegroom, Theagenes of Corinth, fought valiantly in her defense, but was cut down and left for dead; how her aged father and mother collapsed in shock as she was taken away . . .

I couldn't take any more: I jumped to my feet, stomped the ground with my hoof and snorted with fury.

"I will save you, princess!" I was trying to say.

"What's wrong, donkey?" the princess asked softly, trying to soothe me. "Are there fleas in your bedding? I hope not," she continued with a gigantic yawn, "as I'm feeling ever so tired."

And, making a pillow with her hands, she lay down to sleep.

While the princess slept, I looked for our chance to escape. I kept a vigilant watch until the fires died down and the drunken bandits had fallen into their usual slumber. Then I slipped my neck under Charity's waist, lifting her gently onto my back, and tip-toed over the sleeping bandits and out into the night.

The brisk mountain air caused the princess to stir, then awake. "Oh donkey!" she observed with surprise. "You're rescuing me! How brave! How sweet! Take me to my husband's house in Corinth," she began, "and you will be honored – if he's still alive – with your own stall in the royal stables. Never again will you be forced to carry a heavy load. And you shall eat whatever you like."

ROSES! I thought to myself. Flushed with pride and fueled by hope, I picked my way carefully down the mountain towards Corinth with Charity on my back.

By now the sun was rising over the mountains and the princess and I basked in the morning light. Then, just as we were coming round a bend in the trail, we were greeted by a troop of grinning bandits – and they were brandishing swords. We'd been caught!

Up, up, up we climbed, driven by curses and sticks, back to the den of thieves.

CHAPTER VII

The Robber-Bridegroom

LATER THAT afternoon, the bandits assembled in council to determine our punishment. After several equally terrifying suggestions from the floor, a venerable, gray-haired bandit rose to speak.

"Brothers," he began. "My predecessors here have spoken eloquently on the methods of torture we might apply to these runaways, the ass and his lady. While those proposals are each in their own way exquisite, I propose the following: Let's slit open the donkey's paunch and stuff the princess inside. Then," he cackled with delight, "we can leave 'em to rot in the sun, or be eaten alive by vultures and worms!"

WHAT?! For such a minor infraction? Charity and I couldn't believe our ears. We cringed in horror. The bandit council, however, applauded and cheered, and the motion was unanimously passed. No sooner had they pronounced our sentence of torture and death – effective immediately – than a young apprentice bandit broke into their midst with news from Larissa. A hush fell over the cave.

"As you know, brothers," the boy began, "you left me behind in Larissa as a spy to gather information about what the authorities there were planning to do about our attack on the house of Milo. I bring you good news: They do not suspect us at all, but are investigating a house-guest named Prudentius, who was last seen at Milo's the night before the robbery, but mysteriously disappeared, never to be seen or heard from again. In fact, at this very moment, the townspeople are assembling a posse of armed men and dogs to search for this rogue."

The bandits roared hurrah. I almost fainted. My mind had been swimming with thoughts of how happy life had been when I was Prudentius. But now even THAT wish was not safe. I had nowhere to turn. I couldn't even deny these false accusations, beyond uttering a feeble, unintelligible NAW. The old poets were right, I concluded, to declare that Fortune is blind, that she showers her blessings on those who least deserve them and mars the good reputations of innocent people.

But even worse than these musings on the perversity of Fortune was the thought of my more pressing fate: I kept gaz-

34

ing at my belly, trying to imagine myself weirdly pregnant with that poor little girl! I groaned from the very depths of my soul. What had I done to deserve all this?

Suddenly, ANOTHER bandit appeared on the scene. He was quite unlike the others – tall, handsome and strong, but, like them, dressed in rags. He stepped onto a table and, in good Roman fashion, raised his hand to speak.

"BROTHERS," he began in a commanding tone. "I have come to join your ranks. My name is Hymus, son of Hymus the Horrible" – the bandits let out a collective gasp: HYMUS! – "who, as you know, is the King of Thieves. This of course makes me, his son and heir, the Prince. I have been sent by my father to lead you in greater acts of banditry than you have ever known before, and to riches beyond your wildest dreams."

"How do we know you are really a bandit, much less the Prince of Thieves himself, and not a spy?" said an otherwise dimwitted recruit.

Hymus ripped open his tattered cloak and out tumbled a pile of gold coins stamped with the image of Cæsar. The bandits gasped again and began thrusting their hands into the shiny mountain of gold.

"I have brought you this as a down payment in good faith," he said. "There's much more to come. Are you with me?" he shouted.

The bandits again roared hurrah and, forgetting for the

My name is Hymus, son of Hymus the Horrible.

moment our sentence of death, set to preparing a feast in honor of Hymus, son of Hymus the Horrible, while Charity and I cowered in our corner of the cave.

Then the strangest thing happened. During the course of the evening, Hymus, son of Hymus the Horrible, would excuse himself from the feast and sneak us bits of food from his plate. And Charity, much to my surprise and dismay, welcomed each of his gifts with a kiss! Handsome he may be, I thought to myself, but this is a bloodthirsty bandit! Had she so soon forgotten her beloved Theagenes? How fickle! How unsteadfast!

On Hymus's third such visit, he pulled out a knife. Oh no! I thought. First he kisses the girl, and now he's going to KILL her! He lunged with the knife – I closed my eyes – and sliced the rope that bound us together.

"Oh, Theagenes!" Charity cried, giving him the biggest kiss yet. "You're safe and we're saved! But how shall we get past the bandits?"

"I slipped a little something into their wine," Theagenes smiled.

And sure enough, I opened my eyes and saw the whole city of thieves was asleep. We trotted right out of that cave, Charity riding high on my back, and headed for Corinth.

"Are you SURE they're asleep, Theagenes dear?" Charity asked on the way out.

"I made it a double dose," Theagenes replied with a twinkle in his eye. "They won't be awake for days."

On hearing this I made sure to step on a few bandit fingers and toes on my way out.

One Very Naughty Boy

OR EIGHT DAYS and nights we made our merry
way homeward singing songs to Pan along the
road. On the ninth we reached Theagenes's villa
on the outskirts of Corinth. I held my head high
for the approach, the lovely Charity riding side-saddle on
my back.

As we got close to the estate, Charity became alarmed, for
she realized she was wearing just a piece of tattered blanket,
fastened with a pin at the waist and shoulder. (The bandits
had stolen her wedding gown and sold it for a goodly sum.)
This was hardly an appropriate outfit for the grand arrival of
a Princess to her husband's home. "Theagenes, dear," Charity

whimpered with a nervous look on her face, "does this dress make my ass look big?"

I puffed out my chest with pride, thinking she was referring to me.

"No, darling," Theagenes replied. "You're beautiful just as you are."

Charity blushed, and we continued our approach.

Once we arrived, we were welcomed with a magnificent feast, where we exchanged stories of our daring escape. For my part in the adventure, I was hailed as a hero and given the honorific title "Ass of Asses" (of which, I admit, I was immensely proud at the time).

The homecoming celebrations lasted a week, and when they were over I was let out to pasture, just as Charity had promised.

Months passed. I had by this time accustomed myself to the taste of hay. Fortunately, the hay I was given was of the highest quality, with lots of clover in it. It was NOT, however, the happy ending I had imagined. There were no roses anywhere on the property, and the other animals on Theagenes's farm shunned me, jealous of the special treatment I had received. I spent most of each day sulking in my gilded stall.

One day the gardener passed by and peered into the stable. "How is it that a donkey – the 'Ass of Asses' no less," he remarked, looking up at the sign Charity had placed above my head, "is sitting here idle with nothing to do? I could use an ass like you to collect firewood and coping stones for Master Theagenes's fields!"

So saying, the gardener looked over his shoulder, untied my rope, then quite unceremoniously led me back to his hut, where I was put in the charge of his son, a boy about ten years old.

This boy was a MONSTER. He threw a tantrum every time his parents asked him to do something he disliked, and they in turn would always give in to his every whim, which of course only made matters worse. His one chore during the day was to drive me into the forest in search of firewood and stones – the operative word being "drive," for the boy whipped me repeatedly with sticks no matter how hard I worked – and even this he did with disgust.

"You stupid jack-ass!" he would say. "You worthless beast!"

This went on for weeks, the boy maliciously whipping me in the same spot every time until welts began to appear on my haunches. I was better off under the lash of the bandits! I thought to myself.

His cruelty knew no bounds. Whenever we had to cross a river, instead of coaxing me across and helping to steady my load, he hopped right onto my back, with no regard for the weight he was adding to the pile of sticks and stones I was already carrying.

Once, for a wicked thrill, he loaded me up with dry kindling, tossed a hot coal onto my back, and lighted me on fire!

Quid, anxius sim?

That was the last straw. I rolled in a mud puddle to extinguish the blaze, then walked directly over to the boy, turned around and KICKED him into the bushes.

The boy immediately ran home to his parents, dragging me back to the hut by the nose, and accused me of committing grievous acts of violence.

"This donkey's behavior is OUTRAGEOUS," he argued, twisting the facts of the case. "He needs to be fixed."

FIXED? Did they mean – ? GULP! Apparently they did, because I overheard his parents talking about borrowing pincers and a gelding iron from the neighbors.

Well, you can be sure I did my donkey's best to make amends and avert this impending disaster! I whimpered like a puppy, purred like a kitten and tried every other pet trick in the book to win them over. Somehow it worked, and it was agreed that I should be given a second chance.

The next morning I was driven out to the forest as usual, the boy thrashing me harder than ever before. Then, just as I was about to curse my fate, a she-bear bolted out from a nearby cave and took a swipe at the boy. I couldn't believe my eyes! The gods must be rescuing me! I thought.

"Help me, donkey!" the little creature pleaded, narrowly escaping the clutches of the bear. "HELP!"

No pet tricks this time. Instead, I played the part of a dumb ass and looked the other way, pretending not to notice, and slipped away into the forest.

Later that evening, as I was wending my way through the woods, I looked back towards the horizon and could see the boy running across the hillsides of Corinth, still being chased by that glorious bear.

CHAPTER IX

SOLD! to the Eunuch Priest

ES, AS YOU can imagine, I was relieved to be rid of the boy, but it wasn't long before I fell into the hands of another oppressor, for an auctioneer happened to be passing by that morning just as I emerged from the forest.

"Well, well, well, what do we have here?" he smiled broadly, rubbing his greedy hands together. "A donkey with no master? Come with me to Corinth, little fella," he said, "and I'll introduce you to a master with no donkey!" And with an insidious laugh he led me by the nose to the auction block in Corinth.

I was put up for sale that very afternoon with the chickens, oxen and pigs. People poked and prodded me; they peeled my lips apart to inspect my teeth and gums – a very painful procedure, I assure you, not to mention humiliating. One particularly insistent buyer, anxious about the condition of my molars, stuck his WHOLE HAND in my mouth. Well, animal reflexes being what they are, I clamped down hard and caught his fingers between my teeth. *Caveat emptor*, I chuckled to myself: Let the buyer BEWARE!

The man ran off screaming, going out of his way to denounce me to the other bidders in the crowd. Not surprisingly, the biting scandal caused my asking price to drop dramatically. Whereas the auctioneer had been asking forty drachmas, he now reduced the price to an as – a measly Roman penny.

"An ass for an *as*," he shouted. "Only an *as* for an ass!"

Up shot a hand in the crowd. It belonged to a scrawny man with long fingernails, long face, and long hair. As he stepped forward to collect his purchase, I saw that he was wearing a long white robe as well, with a gaudy string of beads around his neck.

"SOLD!" cried the auctioneer, "to the eunuch priest!"

Now I had never been a very religious person. But seeing that I had barely escaped becoming a eunuch myself just the other day, I imagined that I would be joining sympathetic company.

Not so. The grumpy eunuch grabbed me by the scruff of the neck, digging his razor sharp fingernails into my skin, and thrust me on board a merchant ship sailing for Ephesus.

It was a harrowing journey over stormy seas. To make

Such was my brief stint with religion.

matters worse, I had caught a nasty cold on board and had contracted a bad case of the fleas to boot.

When we put to port, the grumpy priest led me sniffling and scratching through the streets of Ephesus to the grotto of the Goddess – the GREAT Goddess, as he called her, throwing himself at the feet of her image. But as far as I was concerned, she was not so much "Great" as just BIG and HEAVY, for as I soon found out, my new job was to carry the marble statue of this massive Goddess on my back while the priests went door to door begging for alms.

A gaggle of priests strapped the Goddess to my back and watched to see how I would react to the Divine Presence. Somehow they managed to interpret my fits of sneezing (due to the cold) and violent shaking (courtesy of the fleas) as a sign of divine possession.

"Look!" they said to one another with glee. "The donkey is dancing in honor of the Goddess!"

So long as I had my cold and my fleas, I was quite an attraction, "dancing" with the priests to the wild sound of cymbals and castanets. The Goddess herself seemed to approve, they said, as she bobbed up and down while I twisted and twirled. My spirited antics earned the eunuchs large sums of money and provisions (all of which, of course, they tossed right onto my back).

My cold lasted for about a week. And I eventually got used to the fleas.

One day, when the priests had danced themselves into a frenzy, I conceived a plan to run away. I gnawed through the leather thongs that held the Great Goddess in place, laid her as gently as I could with a THUD upon the ground, and sauntered off.

Such was my brief stint with religion.

CHAPTER X

Dose to the Grindstone

HERE'S AN ASS supposed to hide on the busy streets of Ephesus, you ask? Nowhere. That's exactly why I was careful not to be seen as I hightailed it out to the countryside, where I thought I'd be safer.

Here again, however, Fortune thwarted my plans: Not far from the city I encountered a miller driving a cart full of ground barley and wheat.

"What a fine looking donkey you are!" he exclaimed. (Toting the Goddess around had apparently done wonders for my physique.) "How's about I take ya home with me n' introduce ya to the family?" he said petting my nose – a bit too roughly for my liking.

The miller tied me up to the rear of his cart, turned around and headed back home. When we arrived at his luxurious house, he instructed his wife to feed me – "but not too much" – and that he would deal with me when he returned from town.

His "family," I soon learned, was a small contingent of slaves he used to mill the grain he sold at a huge profit in town. I was, as it were, a new member by adoption.

When he returned, the miller lowered me down into a deep pit by means of a rope and harness. There, in the middle of this circular space, was a huge millstone that was turned by a long wooden arm. The giant stone wheel was being rolled round and round by men in chains. I shuddered at what I saw.

The men were naked and covered with grime. Each one had been branded on the forehead. Their skin was pasty and pale from lack of sunlight. I felt as if I had descended into the halls of Hades himself and that these men were the ghosts. They came from all over the Empire – Africa, Spain, Bithynia, and Thrace. The miller apparently was no respecter of persons. For the first time in my life as an ass I realized that there were people in this world more wretched than I.

The miller's warden yoked me to a large Spaniard and with the crack of a whip we and ten other slaves strained to push the millstone on its monotonous course. For weeks and weeks, with little water or food, we went round and round, wearing a rut in the ground underfoot.

My tired legs were quivering all the time from this arduous work, so it took me a while to realize what was happening

I had descended into Hades.

that wonderful day when Fortune reversed herself and finally came to my aid: There was a groan from the depths of the earth. We all brought the millstone to a halt and listened, trembling with fear. Then the ground seemed to shift and the walls of the pit buckled and swayed. The men shouted "LOOK OUT!" as the wall in front of me started to crumble. It was an earthquake!

Suddenly, one side of the pit collapsed – as luck would have it, directly on top of the warden's station. When the dust had settled, we could see that the resulting pile of rocks had formed a miraculous ramp to the world above.

I broke loose from my yoke and pawed through the rubble until I found the warden's keys. I brought them to the Spaniard with my teeth and he proceeded to set himself and the other captives free.

Out of the pit we climbed, arm in arm, shielding our eyes from the bright light of the sun. When we reached the top, we heard muffled voices nearby. We clambered over to the sound and saw that the quake had formed a huge crevice in the earth. And there, down below, were the miller, his wife, and the remains of their fancy house.

"Stuck in a hole of their own making, I should say," one of the men observed. We all heartily agreed.

The men thanked me profusely for finding the keys. "FREE AT LAST!" they cheered.

Then, with tears in our eyes, we all said good-bye to our

yoke mates. Each man set off on his own journey home – to Africa, Spain, Bithynia, and Thrace. I too longed to return home, to Rome, and to my former self. But my odyssey was not yet through.

CHAPTER XI

The Die Is Cast

SCARCELY HAD my newly found friends departed than I heard someone shouting behind me.

"You there, HALT!"

I looked up, and there, running straight at me in his hobnailed sandals, cuirass, and helmet, was a Roman soldier.

"In the name of the Emperor, I say, HALT!"

Just as he uttered the word HALT, the bumpkin tripped over a rock and went flying headlong through the air. I watched as the clumsy soldier and his clattering armor both tumbled into a heap in front of me.

The soldier rose awkwardly to his feet, trying not to look embarrassed, brushed the dust off his arms, and straightened his helmet.

"I hereby commandeer you," he began in a soldiering tone, pretending to read from a papyrus scroll (which I noticed was

upside down), "in accordance with Roman Law . . . let's see . . .
yes, Chapter IX, Section VII of the Domesticated Animal
Code, to carry the equipment of the honorable centurion,
Decimus Verissimus Stultus – that's me," he looked up with a
winning smile – "to the port city of Ephesus for his return
journey to Rome."

Then, stuffing the scroll into his cuirass, he heaved his
armor and a large sack of provisions onto my back: THUMP!
My knees buckled under the load, but by now I was used to
this routine.

From the centurion's incessant chattering on the road
back to Ephesus I gathered that the Emperor himself was
preparing to return to Rome from his victories in Germania
and that Decimus would be participating in his triumphal
procession.

Now THIS appeared to be good news! The centurion
would be my armed escort home! I relished the thought as we
plodded along toward Ephesus.

On our way into town we practically bumped into my former masters, the eunuch priests, who were dancing a jig at
the door of a rich man. I lowered my head so as not to be seen.
I was determined to let nothing – not even the Great Goddess
herself – interfere with my passageway home.

We made our way to the docks, climbed aboard a merchant vessel and set sail that evening for Rome.

It was a whale of a ship and I was lodged in its bowels with

We made our way to the docks and set sail for Rome.

the rats, the stowaways and slaves, while on deck Decimus played dice with the captain and crew.

I watched him through a crack in the floor.

"*Alea iacta est!*" he would chortle jokingly after every roll of the dice – "The die is cast!" But unlike the great Julius Cæsar of yesteryore, this soldier's gambling fell far short of victory.

We sailed for three days and three moonlit nights upon the shining sea. By the time we reached Brundisium, Decimus was deeply in debt. When he finally marched himself down into the hold to fetch me, I could see in his eyes that the news was not so good after all.

"Donkey," he said resolutely. "I'm sorry. I'm going to have to sell you."

And so, to pay off his debts, Decimus Verissimus Stultus, the honorable, lovable, yet stupid centurion, sold me to two brothers, both gourmet chefs for a local magistrate.

I liked Decimus and would miss him. But at least my new masters had culture, I thought to myself. The clean crisp air of Brundisium also helped lift my spirits.

The brothers took me straight to market and loaded me up with the fruits of Empire: olives and sausages, apples and cheese; lentils and garlic and chickens and salt; basil, pistachios, honey, and bread; peppers and ONIONS and WALNUTS and GRAPES!

Italians, I now remembered, know how to eat! I could barely contain myself, as I carried this cornucopia home.

He's practically H U M A N!

CHAPTER XII

Sweets and Savories

"N o I DID NOT!"

"Yes you did!"

"No, I did NOT!"

"Yes, you DID!"

"*Non!*"

"*Sic!*"

"*Non!!*"

"*Sic!!*"

The brothers argued like this all the way home, haggling over who had left the money-purse at the fish monger's stall. And no wonder they were upset, because no sooner had we arrived at the house – a three-mile journey, at least – than we had to go all the way back to the market to get it.

The brothers were twins. One was called Castor, the other Pollux, and they were constantly at each other's throats.

They would argue about EVERYTHING: Which is the better condiment, salt or pepper? Which emperor had the bigger nose, Caligula or Nero? Who was the nastier gladiator, Tarquinius or Morbo? Is that glass of wine half-empty or half-full?

Their squabbling was tiresome, but, OH, by Jove, these boys could COOK!

Castor specialized in sauces, Pollux in pastries. They worked from dawn to dusk concocting delectables for Avidius, a good-natured gourmand and the wealthy mayor of Brundisium.

Here, I must confess, after so many trials and tribulations as an ass, my human nature got the better of me: While the brothers cooked by day, I would sneak into the kitchen at night and snatch delicious bits of food. The brothers, so intent on bickering, blamed each other for the theft, in spite of some tell-tale signs:

"Don't you think the donkey's getting FAT?" Castor remarked one day.

"No, I wouldn't say FAT," Pollux replied. "ROTUND, perhaps, but definitely not FAT."

Eventually, however – and perhaps for the first time in their lives – the twins came to an agreement: If neither of THEM was responsible for the missing morsels, they should stay up late in order to catch the REAL thief red-handed.

That night, not knowing about their secret pact, I broke into the kitchen as usual, sat myself down amidst the sweets and savories and started to eat. Like the Lotus-Eaters of long ago, I gave no thought to returning home, no thought to roses – the true food of my salvation – no thought at all except for the wonderful dishes that lay before me.

Castor and Pollux stormed into the kitchen. I looked up, wide-eyed with guilt-ridden surprise, my muzzle covered with crumbs.

"AHA!" the brothers cried in unison. "It's the DONKEY!"

The next day I was dragged by the ears to the town hall.

"Avidius, Sir! This ass has been stealing your desserts!" Pollux exclaimed.

"And your dinners!" added Castor.

"Why, he has good taste then, doesn't he?" Avidius laughed. "Perhaps we should teach this smart ass a lesson and invite him to a proper dinner party. Then we'll see how truly smart he is!"

This idea so amused Avidius that I was specially groomed for the occasion and taught to eat while reclining on a couch, as all good Romans do. I even learned how to hold a goblet with my hoof.

That night I was the center of attention, reclining there at table next to Avidius with my goblet in hand. His guests were very impressed.

"That's one smart ass you've got there, Avidius," one guest observed.

"He's practically HUMAN!" remarked another.

The evening wore on, and I was quite enjoying myself and all this flattery.

After dessert, Avidius stood up and called for music.

He clapped his hands and a band of musicians stepped to the front of the room. The sound of castanets and cymbals reminded me of my days in Ephesus and, momentarily forgetting myself (having drunk by now two goblets of wine), I stood up on my haunches and started to DANCE.

My whirling dervish received a round of applause and cups brimming with wine were raised in my honor.

"BRAVO!" the guests shouted, "BRAVO!"

"Now this sure beats politics!" Avidius exclaimed as he considered my potential for financial success.

In fact, the very next day he resigned his position as mayor, purchased me from the twins for one hundred talents, and took my show on the road.

That's what you get for being a smart ass.

Circus Sideshow

VIDIUS, it turns out, was quite an entrepreneur. In the beginning it was simply a matter of me performing my party tricks – reclining at table, drinking from the goblet, and dancing the dervish – in various towns across Italy: Tarentum, Capua, Naples. Avidius would set up a little booth decorated like a dining room in the town forum and charge ten *denarii* per person to see me perform.

But soon he was on to bigger and better things. Actually, I would say things got out of control, for Avidius, the entrepreneur, reinvented himself as an ARTIST.

First, he wrote and produced a little ballet number in which I starred as Pegasus, the winged horse of heaven, and he as the hero Bellerophon. I was fitted out with a pair of mechanical wings and Avidius rode on my back through the air, miming the motions of Bellerophon as he slew the monster Chimæra.

When he grew tired of this routine, he had ME play the Chimæra. For this role I had to wear an impossibly hot and sweaty costume. The Chimæra's head, of course, is that of a lion. For this I wore a huge lion mask made from papier mâché. The Chimæra's body is that of a goat. (My own body was deemed sufficiently squat and goat-like to represent this.) And her tail is shaped like a dragon's. For this, Avidius hooked me up to a contraption of small interlocking hoops, over which he stretched the skin of a spotted snake.

The worst part about the role of Chimæra, however, was the moment in the play when Avidius would cut off my head. I cringed every time, fearing that one day he might miss the papier mâché lion mask and accidentally lop off my nose.

We even performed that part of the myth where proud Bellerophon rides Pegasus to heaven but is thrown from his mount when Pegasus is stung by a horsefly sent by Jove himself to punish the impudence of the rider. To recreate this scene of high drama, Avidius hired a boy in the crowd to fire stones at my flank with a slingshot.

"*Ars gratia artis,*" Avidius would say, trying to console me when I made known my displeasure with this stunt. But was THIS, I protested, what is meant by art for art's sake?!

Avidius decided to take our show to Rome, where, he

Ars gratia artis.

insisted, we would find fortune and fame. He devised a new skit for us to perform: *The Trojan Horse*. You can guess what part I was going to play.

As it happened, our arrival at Rome coincided with the Emperor's homecoming parade. And, as you might expect, HIS production put OURS to shame.

CHAPTER XIV

My Fair Lady

HE STREETS were lined with well-wishers,
senators, and trumpeters. The Emperor
himself rode slowly through the streets to the Capitol in a
chariot of gold. Following in his train were dancers, jugglers,
musicians, and jesters. Captured German soldiers, sham-
bling along in shackles and chains, brought up the rear of his
entourage, followed by the legions of Rome. I even thought I
saw Decimus hobbling along with the troops. The sheer spectacle of it all took my breath away. I felt certain that there
would be roses at this parade, and that my chance to return to
my former self was at hand. I waited expectantly, full of hope.

The triumphal procession lasted for HOURS. Then, just
as the Emperor's chariot passed by where Avidius and I were
standing, a flock of young girls stepped forward and showered

the victorious Emperor with flowers. My heart raced! I pushed my way to the front of the crowd to get a better look.

They were daisies. My heart sank once again to the pit of my stomach, all my hopes dashed. Crestfallen, I returned to my place at the back of the crowd.

I want to be Prudentius, again! I cried, my eyes welling up with tears. I cannot go on like this, the plaything of Fortune! Cruel, blind Fortune! I'm sorry that I lied to get into Milo's wife's room. I'm sorry I was so cocksure, greedy, and selfish. Get me out of this ass's hide! Please, I want to be Prudentius again!

Just then I had a most rare vision. I heard a voice beckoning me: "Prudentius," it called. "Prudentius."

It was a woman's voice, the sweetest, most beautiful, peaceful sound I had ever heard.

"Eat roses from my bosom, Prudentius."

"What do you mean?" I asked, perplexed, gazing up into to the sky. "Who are you?"

I sensed a presence, a feeling of pure love, as if I was hearing the voice of my own mother, gone these many years. I turned around and there before me stood a magnificent woman, a goddess, surely, I thought to myself. Her face was radiant, with full red lips and bright green eyes. Her long black hair was interwoven with flowers and fell loosely in curls about her shoulders. She wore a golden crown, which had an embossed design of sheaves of wheat on either side

Eat roses from my bosom.

and a flat round disc in the center like a mirror – an image of
the Moon – that shone with a silvery light. Her linen mantle
was deep blue, the color of the sea, and cascaded over her
body in a thousand intricate pleats. Around her waist she
wore a saffron-colored sash. Her skin was milky white, and
her breath smelled sweet and delicious – of Arabian spices,
frankincense, and myrrh.

"Eat roses from my bosom, Prudentius."

"There are no roses on your bosom, My Lady," I replied,
and, believe me, I had looked closely.

"Return to the parade," she whispered in my ear. "There
you will see a procession in my honor. You will find all the
roses you could ever want."

"Who are you, Goddess?" I asked again, awestruck by this
serene apparition.

"I am the Mother of the Universe," she replied. "The
Queen of Heaven. Goddess of many names and guises. Some
call me Juno, some Venus, Diana, Persephone – I am all of
them. They are all of me. But I am known to mortal men and
gods also as Isis, the mistress and patron deity of Egypt. I
have seen your sufferings, Prudentius, and have come to take
pity on you. In return, I ask that you pledge yourself to me –
pledge yourself to love, and to wisdom."

"I'll do the best I can, My Lady, I promise!" and off I
bounded, back to the parade. "Thank you!" I said, looking
back, but she was already gone.

As I trotted back to the parade, the bustling activity around me was reduced to slow motion. I saw my whole life flash before my eyes. I began to feel dizzy, and strange faces in the crowd began to look strangely familiar. There was Milo, I thought, and Charity; and that foul child who lighted me on fire; and the miller, the eunuchs, the twins; even the rough auctioneer!

I pushed my way to the front of the crowd and staggered into the street. There, bringing up the rear of the Emperor's triumph, was a small procession of devotees of Isis, who were carrying her statue through the streets, and there, around her neck, nestled in that glorious bosom, was a thick garland of red and yellow roses.

I ran up to her image, devoured a mouthful, then another, and another. The moist, delicate petals burst in my mouth like sunshine on a stormy day. As I ate, the world began to look larger and larger, and I to feel smaller and smaller. POOF! My hooves became hands. POOF! My hairy hide became flesh once again. "YES!" I cried with no longer unspeakable joy. I had returned to my former self a changed man. In fact, I caught my reflection in the mirror on the Isis statue's crown and saw that, much to my surprise, I had turned into – who could believe it? – a BOY!

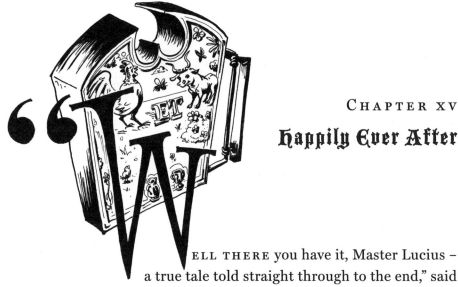

CHAPTER XV

Happily Ever After

"ELL THERE you have it, Master Lucius – a true tale told straight through to the end," said Prudentius with a perfectly innocent grin on his face.

"BAH!" Cylindrius burst out, shaking his head in disbelief. "Lies, I tell you, LIES! Asses? Isis? BAH!"

"True or not, Cylindrius, that story belongs in a book," I mused, completely enthralled by this supernatural tale. "Someone ought to write it down. But tell me, Prudentius, is that really the end?"

"Actually, no. There's one more chapter.

"When I realized I had been magically transformed into a boy," Prudentius continued, "my first reaction was dismay: 'Do I really have to be eleven again? I hated being eleven.' But Isis appeared again and consoled me:

74

"'Most people are only young once, Prudentius, but they stay immature forever. You've become young again and have been given a unique second chance to make the most of your life. Besides,' she added with a smile, 'given all that you've been through, you'll be twice as smart as most eleven-year-olds.'

"The Goddess took my hand and led me to a large mansion near the Capitol. She knocked on the door and then vanished from sight.

"A woman answered the door. I noticed that her eyes were red and swollen and that her cheeks were stained with tears. When I asked her what was wrong, she told me that she and her husband had lost their only child to an illness that very day, a boy about my age. When I told them that I, too, had lost my parents in a shipwreck, she smiled through her tears, stroked my hair, and said that Fate must have brought us together. So she and her husband took me in, treated me as their own son, and sponsored my education. In fact, I'm traveling this very road to Larissa today in order to begin my studies with the great philosopher Demetrius. Cylindrius here is my chaperone."

"TUTOR!" objected Cylindrius. "And that story of yours is completely preposterous! The first thing Demetrius had better teach you is to tell the truth!"

"You see, Master Lucius," said Prudentius, politely ignoring this outburst, "I now realize after living the life of an ass that

My dinner debt now was due.

none of us should take anything for granted. Things in this world are not always what they seem. And practically anything can happen to anybody. Isis was right: I was self-centered. So I'm taking her advice and making the most of this strange second chance. I have pledged myself to love, and to wisdom."

"Yeah, he's studying to become a WISE ass!" chuckled Cylindrius, thoroughly amused by his own joke. "So when's dinner?" he added abruptly, licking his lips and wringing his hands.

I looked up and saw that we had indeed arrived at Larissa and that my dinner debt now was due.

But dinner was the last thing on my mind: As we approached the inn, I felt nervously in the folds of my toga for that sparkling letter of introduction that I, too, carried from Demeas to Milo, and wondered what kind of ass I might have made of myself had I not heard the tale of Prudentius. I also thought of the book I would write. Where to begin?

Exordior. Thessaliam ex negotio petebam . . .

THE END

or, rather, just the BEGINNING

Afterword

A note on this version for librarians, teachers, scholars,
and extremely intelligent children

THE ORIGINAL *Golden Ass*, of which this book is a reworking, was composed in Latin by Lucius Apuleius around A.D. 150. Apuleius was a native of Madaura, North Africa (modern M'Daourouch in Algeria), but he was related on his mother's side to the great Greek biographer and philosopher Plutarch. His native language was probably Punic (a Semitic language akin to Hebrew) and his second tongue was Greek. Latin was a third language that he only acquired when he moved to Rome as a young man to study rhetoric, philosophy, and law. Consequently, Apuleius's Latin is idiosyncratic and highly stylized, as is often the case with writers of artistic prose who work in a non-native language. (Take Vladimir Nabokov, for example, or Joseph Conrad.) Yet his style and narrative technique is captivating in its own way: It is ornate, allusive, and packed with puns and other sound effects. To be able to read Apuleius in the original is one of the best reasons to learn some Latin, even if your first language is Punic.

79

Apuleius's tale of the comic misadventures of a young man who accidently turns himself into an ass was called "golden" in antiquity because, in the view of ancient readers, his version was, as it were, The Greatest Ass Story Ever Told. There were others. In fact, fragments of two such have survived in Greek but they fall flat by comparison, suggesting that antiquity's verdict was justified. The present version for modern readers of all ages is a continuation of this tradition of creative adaptation of "the ass story," and my hope is that it will take its place alongside Apuleius's own.

While this retelling follows Apuleius rather closely in its general outline and in many details, there are some departures. First and foremost, besides changing some names, adding a few characters here and there, and omitting, trimming or otherwise adapting scenes, I have made the protagonist a boy – Prudentius – and transferred to him the experiences of Apuleius's hero, Lucius, whom Prudentius actually meets in the first chapter and to whom he tells his tale. The experiences of Prudentius, then, mirror and anticipate the experiences of the "real" Lucius of Apuleius. When at the end of our story Lucius says that Prudentius's tale would make a terrific book, that someone should write it down, that's an oblique way of suggesting that an outlandish tale told by a twelve-year-old boy could very well have been the inspiration for one of the greatest comic novels in the history of literature. Children are, after all, some of the world's best fabulists.

In any event, readers of this version are left where Apuleius's story begins. Curious readers who want to experience the whole of Apuleius's original can do so in several excellent translations. Robert Graves's is a personal favorite. P. G. Walsh's translation for the Oxford World Classics series is also lively. (But let the reader beware: there are some bawdy R-rated scenes in the original that I deleted for this PG-13 version.)

The biggest change from the original in this adaptation is the omission of the tale of Cupid and Psyche, perhaps the most famous interlude in *The Golden Ass*. In Apuleius, the story of Cupid and Psyche is told in the bandits' cave by an old woman to Charity in order to cheer her up. Why leave out such a well-known part of *The Golden Ass*? In short, it's too long. And too digressive: It was clearly an add-on inserted by Apuleius to the ass-story template. However, it is worth a nod here because it is, in essence, an intriguing early version of the Cinderella story – with a philosophical twist.

A princess named Psyche (which means "soul" in Greek), the youngest of three sisters, is so beautiful that the people of the land pay no attention to the goddess Venus and offer prayers and worship to Psyche instead. Venus is enraged and sends her son Cupid (the god of love), to shoot one of his arrows at Psyche to punish her by making her fall in love with an ogre. But when Cupid sets eyes on Psyche he falls in love with her himself. All the while invisible, he arranges to have

Psyche transported to his celestial palace and visits her bed every night. The one condition of their relationship is that she cannot look upon his face. Psyche is supremely happy in her new celestial home, but eventually grows homesick, so Cupid allows her to return to the world of mortals to visit her family. She tells her sisters about her relationship with an unseen god, but they don't believe her. They are, like Venus, jealous of her good fortune and beauty, so they plant a seed of doubt in Psyche's mind that her lover is not a god at all, but a monster. Why else would he hide his face? Psyche resolves to settle the question the next time her lover visits her chamber. As she holds up a lamp to get a glimpse of Cupid while he's sleeping, some hot oil drips on him and he wakes up. Because Psyche broke faith in the terms of her agreement with Cupid, she is forced by Venus to perform various labors, going even so far as the Underworld (to fetch a box of beauty from the goddess of the Dead, Proserpina) in her toils, all of which she completes successfully with the help of various forces and creatures of Nature (e.g., an ant, an eagle, a river). Cupid, meanwhile, with Psyche gone, becomes depressed and begs Jupiter, king of the gods, to release her from the labors imposed by his mother. Jupiter agrees and declares that Cupid and Psyche be married. Psyche is swept up to Mount Olympus and given a drink mixed with ambrosia, the food of the gods, whereupon she becomes immortal. She gives birth to a daughter, Voluptas ("pleasure" or "desire" in Latin) and they all live happily ever after. (T. Motley's illustration to Chapter 15 alludes to parts of the Cupid and Psyche story in the figures he portrays in the tavern windows.)

It is clear that Apuleius intended this sprawling tale-within-a-tale, embedded as it is in the very center of his narrative, to reflect on the outer story of Lucius's transformation into an ass. Like Psyche, Apuleius's Lucius lets curiosity get the better of him: He sees what he should not have seen and so has to expiate his mistake through a series of labors. Of course, these are largely comical adventures, but the Cupid and Psyche story adds a certain earnestness to the whole narrative, for, ultimately, it is an allegory on the striving of the Soul to be united with divine Love. Many of the tale's themes are drawn from the philosophy of Plato, to which Apuleius himself was partial. Plato distinguishes between common, terrestrial love and a divine, pure, eternal variety. Our souls, according to Platonic philosophy, ultimately seek the latter. We travel through life in a body, too often enslaved to its passions and distracted by its appetites, while our better selves, our souls, yearn to return to their heavenly home beyond the dross of this mortal life. In *The Golden Ass*, for the protagonist to have the body of a donkey suggests just how low we humans can slip.

At the end of the original *Golden Ass*, Apuleius's Lucius, like our Prudentius, is transformed back into human form by the intervention of the Egyptian goddess Isis. Both characters are redeemed by grace from a state of misery and suffering, which is partly deserved, and partly the result of mere Fortune or Chance. In Apuleius's time cults of various foreign deities (i.e., not Greek or Roman) attracted many devotees in Greco-Roman cities throughout the Mediterranean. Unlike Roman State religion and the mythology of the Olympian pantheon, these cults and their gods offered psychological transcendence over the whims of Fortune, salvation in the Hereafter, and a set of exotic rituals and a community of worshippers here on earth. In Apuleius's *Golden Ass*, Lucius, in gratitude for the grace shown to him by Isis, becomes a priest in her cult and returns to Rome to practice law and behave himself. In the final chapter of his novel he speaks eloquently, and with conviction, of his conversion; in particular of the joy and serenity that his communion with Isis provides. At this point more than any other in the text one gets the sense that Apuleius's tale of Lucius (Apuleius's own first name, after all) is to some degree autobiographical. Some have even seen the novel as a tract for Isiac religion.

The twist in my version is that Prudentius, once transformed, returns from young adulthood to the relative innocence of boyhood. He is given "a strange second chance" to make better life-choices going forward. Wisely, he decides to study philosophy. In both my and the original version Isis emerges as a compassionate, nurturing mother figure, a *dea ex machina*, who makes things right. It is not at all surprising that much of her iconography and many of her attributes were later transferred to the Virgin Mary. To my own way of thinking, however, Apuleius's Isis is perhaps closest to the glorious Blue Fairy in *Pinocchio*, a book and film that in fact owes a considerable debt to *The Golden Ass*. Her injunction to a young puppet who has made a jackass of himself – "prove yourself to be brave, truthful and unselfish" in order to become truly human (i.e., "a real boy") – is a worthy motto in any age, for any age. Apuleius, I think, would not have disapproved.